Written by
Julia Donaldson

Illustrated by
Rebecca Cobb

The Everywhere Bear

MACMILLAN CHILDREN'S BOOKS

With her blue pointy shoes and her hair in a bun,
Mrs McAllister teaches Class One.

That's Ollie and Holly and Josie and Jay,
Leo and Theo and April and May,
Billy and Lily and little Lee Wu,
Daisy and Maisie, and Matt (who is new),
Hanahazala, Callum and Clare,
Kevin and Bev – and the Everywhere Bear.

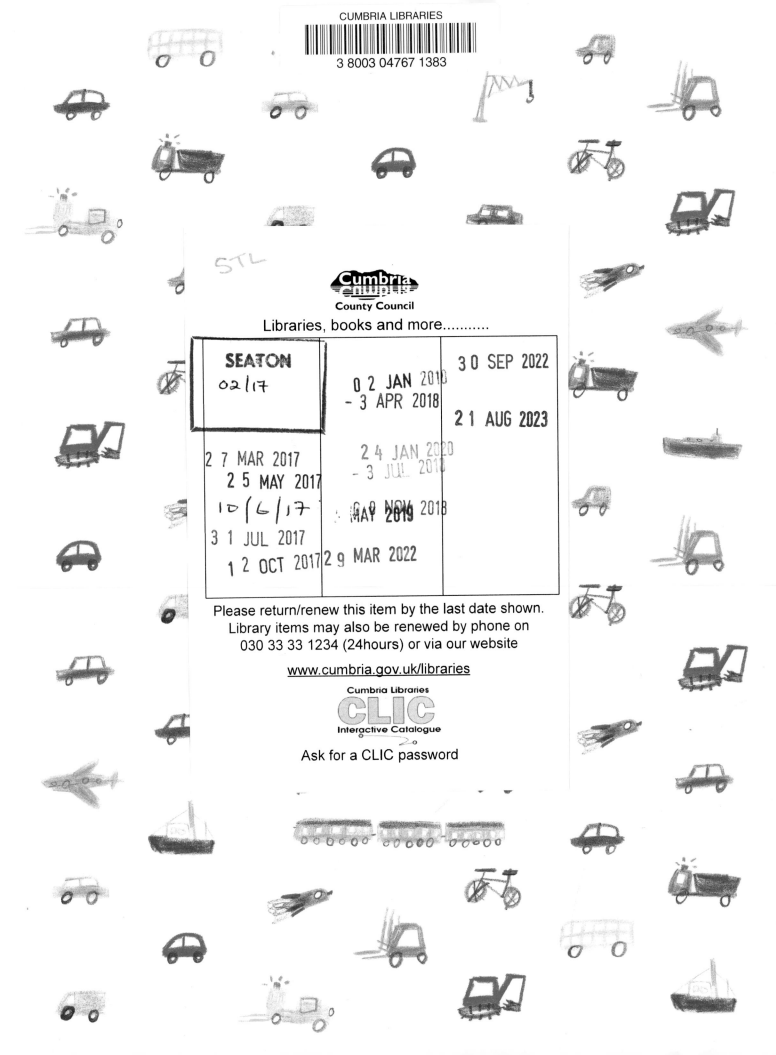

The Everywhere Bear has a home on a shelf
But he doesn't spend very much time by himself,
For each boy and girl in the class is a friend
And he goes home with one of them every weekend.
On Mondays they carry him back to Class One
And tell all the others the things that he's done.

He has bus rides with April

April

May

and horse rides with May.

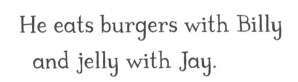

Billy

Jay

He eats burgers with Billy
and jelly with Jay.

With Lee Wu he's a pirate, with Kevin a king,
And Callum and Clare push him high on the swing.
He bounces with Bev and does handstands with Holly.
He likes playing football with Maisie and Ollie.
He always makes dens when he goes home with Daisy.
At Lily's they let him be lovely and lazy.

Lee Wu

Kevin

Clare and Callum

Bev

Holly

Daisy

Lily

Maisie and Ollie

Hanahazala

Leo and Theo

Josie

With Leo and Theo he tinkles a tune.
With Hanahazala he goes to the moon.
With Josie he whizzes about in a chair.
No wonder they call him the Everywhere Bear.

One rainy Monday the new boy called Matt
Was splashing to school when he spotted a cat,
And when he bent over to give it a cuddle
The Everywhere Bear tumbled into a puddle.

Just round the corner, a driver called Pete
Sat in a van painting stripes on the street.

Matt got to school
  and sat down on his chair.
He opened his bag . . .
  and the Bear wasn't there!

Nobody knew that the poor little fellow,
Just like the street, had been painted bright yellow.
Nobody saw when a river of rain
Washed him and whooshed him head first down a drain.

And no one was there when the Bear with the stripe,
Dirty and dizzy, splashed out of the pipe.

The water was wild and the weather was wet
When Jim, Jeff and Jonathan hauled in their net.
Waves rocked the boat and a storm filled the air.
None of them noticed the Everywhere Bear.

Back in the harbour, Mohammed Hussein
Lifted the fish off the boat with his crane.

"Give me two boxes," said old Mrs Bishop.
And she cheerfully wheeled them away to her fish shop.

She started unpacking, then muttered, "That's odd.
There's a bear wrapped in seaweed between these two cod!"

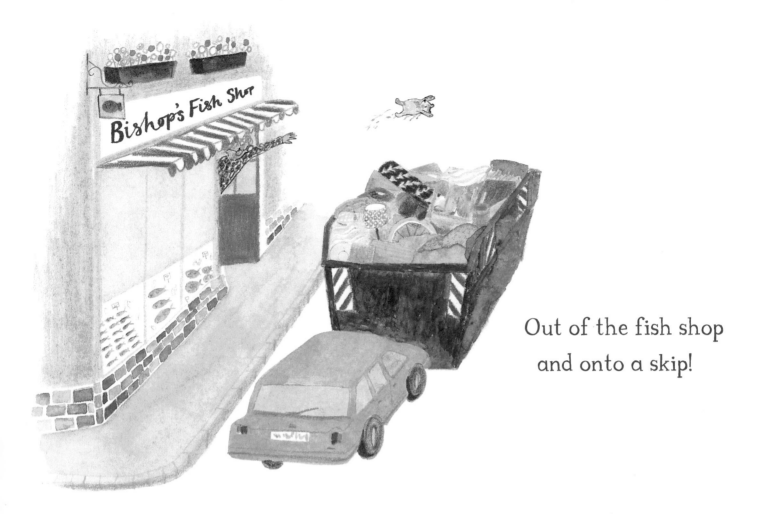

Out of the fish shop
and onto a skip!

Into a lorry,
and off to the tip!

"Aha!" squawked a seagull called Solomon Shriek.
"I smell fish!" - and he picked up the Bear in his beak.

They flew over treetops and over the town,
And the Bear saw his school when he dared to look down.

Then Solomon perched
on the roof of a shop.
"This isn't a fish!"
- and

he

let

the

Bear

drop.

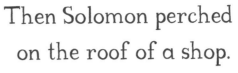

Then a very kind lady called Bethany Burke
Picked the Bear up on her way into work . . .

Each Friday morning Class One pays a visit
To one of their favourite places. Where is it?

The library! Jay finds a book about stars.
Josie finds one about buses and cars.

Billy likes aliens and Lily likes lizards.
Hanahazala is keener on wizards.

Finally everyone's chosen a book.
They queue at the counter; then Matt cries out "Look!"
April and May and the others say, "Where?"
"Behind you! He's there! It's the Everywhere Bear!"

Then they carry him happily home to Class One,
Saying "Where have you been, Bear,
and what have you done?"

The Bear never talks, but he smiles to himself,
And thinks, as he settles back down on his shelf,
"I've been in a puddle, I've been down a drain,
I've been in a boat and I've been in a crane.
I've been in a shop and I've been on a skip.
I've been on a lorry, I've been on a tip.
I've been in a beak and I've been in the air.
No wonder they call me the Everywhere Bear!"

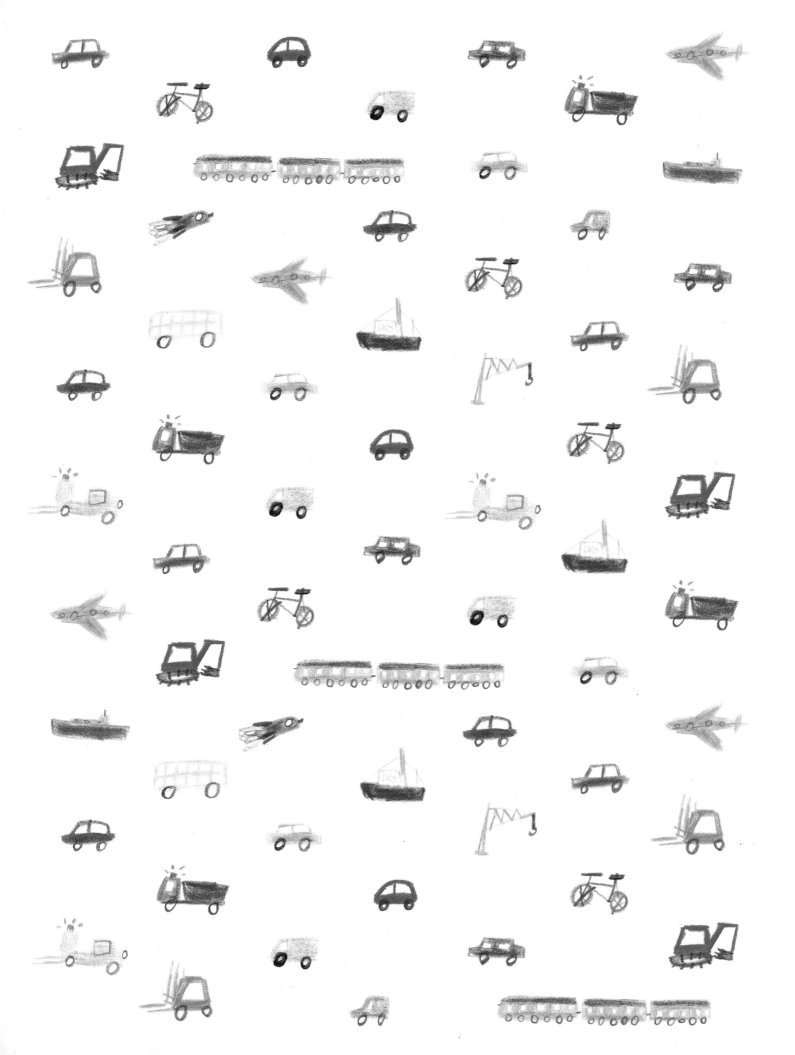